SOFIA MARTINEZ

Picture Perfect

by Jacqueline Jules

illustrated by Kim Smith

PICTURE WINDOW BOOKS
a capstone imprint

Sofia Martinez is published by
Picture Window Books, a Capstone Imprint
1710 Roe Crest Drive
North Mankato, MN 56003
www.capstonepub.com

Library of Congress Cataloging-in-Publication Data
Jules, Jacqueline, 1956- author.
Picture perfect / by Jacqueline Jules ; illustrated by
Kim Smith.
pages cm. -- (Sofia Martinez)

Summary: Sofia feels that because she looks so much
like her older sisters, nobody notices her — so when
school picture day comes around she comes up with a
way to stand out.

ISBN 978-1-4795-5773-8 (library binding)
ISBN 978-1-4795-5777-6 (pbk.)
ISBN 978-1-4795-6205-3 (ebook)

1. Sisters — Juvenile fiction. 2. Spanish Americans —
Juvenile fiction. 3. Photographs — Juvenile
fiction. 4. Identity (Psychology) — Juvenile fiction.
[1. Sisters — Fiction. 2. Hispanic Americans —
Fiction. 3. Photographs — Fiction. 4. Identity —
Fiction.] I. Smith, Kim, 1986- illustrator. II. Title.
PZ7.J92947Pj 2015   [E]—dc23
                                2014024244

Designer: Kay Fraser

Printed in the United States of America in
Stevens Point, Wisconsin.
092014   008479WZS15

TABLE OF CONTENTS

CHAPTER 1

Picture Trick

Sofia stared at the school pictures from last year. They were lined up on top of the piano.

"I knew it!" Sofia said. "We are all wearing blue!"

All three Martinez sisters had long dark hair, brown eyes, and a few freckles.

Sofia was the youngest sister.

Luisa was in the middle. Elena was

the oldest.

Everyone said the girls looked

alike. This annoyed Sofia. She

wanted to stand out.

"I have a plan," Sofia said.

Sofia put her picture in Elena's frame. She put Elena's picture in her frame.

"¡Perfecto!" Sofia said.

Just then, her mom walked into the living room.

"¡Mira!" Sofia said. "We all wore blue last year."

"How cute," Mamá said with a smile.

That was not what Sofia wanted to hear. She waited for her mom to see the switch. She didn't notice.

Sofia folded her arms. She was going to have to work harder to get someone to notice her picture trick.

CHAPTER 2

The Crazy Bow

That night all the family came for dinner. Sofia loved seeing her cousins, especially baby Mariela.

Mariela wore a big bow in her hair. Everyone kept talking about that crazy bow.

"She looks like a birthday present!" Papá laughed.

Abuela couldn't stop smiling.

"Niña hermosa."

Tío Miguel took a bunch of

pictures and showed everyone.

Baby Mariela was hogging all the attention. Sofia knew she had to get her family closer to the piano. Then they would see the picture switch.

"¿Mamá?" Sofia asked. "Will you play a song for us?"

"I would love to," Mamá said.

Mamá was a piano teacher. She knew lots of songs, and the Martinez family loved to sing.

Everyone gathered around the piano and sang and sang. Sofia waited and waited.

Nobody noticed the picture switch. Sofia did not feel like singing anymore. She went and sat down. Her papá followed her.

"¿Qué pasa?" Papá asked Sofia. "You are always the loudest singer in our group."

"Not tonight," Sofia said. "I am too sad to sing."

"¿Por qué?" Papá asked.

"No one ever notices me," Sofia said sadly.

"My sweet Sofia," Papá said. "There are a lot of people here. Everyone can't always pay attention to you."

"Why not? I want to stand out!" Sofia said.

Papá laughed. "Like baby Mariela and that giant bow?"

"¡Exactamente!" Sofia said.

Sofia felt better. Thanks to **Papá**, she had a new idea.

She gave her **papá** a big hug and went back to the piano to sing.

CHAPTER 3

The New Picture

On Monday morning, Sofia got up early. It was picture day. She needed her cousin Hector's help before pictures. She ran across the yard to talk to him. They didn't have much time.

"I can help you, but we have to be quiet," Hector said.

Hector and Sofia tiptoed into baby Mariela's room.

"Don't forget to give this back," he whispered. "It's my mom's favorite one."

"Gracias, Hector," Sofia said.

She ran back home to finish
getting ready. It was a big day,
and she wanted everything to be
perfect. Sofia couldn't wait to take
her school picture this year!

* * *

The day school pictures were delivered, Sofia ran home. Mamá and Tía Carmen were talking and drinking coffee in the kitchen.

Sofia rushed past them.

"What's the big hurry, Sofia?"
Mamá asked.

Sofia went straight to her frame
on the piano. She slipped her new
school picture inside.

She jumped when **Mamá** and **Tía** Carmen walked in. Her sisters were right behind them.

"What do you think?" Sofia asked. She was very proud.

When her sisters saw the picture, they started laughing.

But Sofia didn't care. She loved her picture. Mariela's big bow made her stand out.

"Oh, Sofia!" Mamá said, smiling. "¡Muy hermosa!"

"How did you get baby Mariela's bow?" Tía Carmen asked.

"Hector helped me," Sofia said. "No te preocupes. I already put it back in its spot."

"Thank you," Tía Carmen said. "And the bow looks perfect in your picture."

"Thank you!" Sofia said.

"Why did you wear the bow, Sofia?" Mamá asked.

Sofia told them how she had mixed up the old school pictures.

"No one even noticed," Sofia said, frowning. "I looked too much like Elena."

"Not any more," Mamá said.

"¡Yo sé!" Sofia giggled. "Now my picture is special."

"It always was," Mamá said. "All three of my girls are special."

She put her arms out to give Sofia, Luisa, and Elena a big hug.

"Te quiero, Mamá," Sofia said.

"Te quiero, Sofia," Mamá said.

Spanish Glossary

abuela — grandma

exactamente — exactly

gracias — thank you

mamá — mom

mira — look

muy hermosa — very beautiful

niña hermosa — beautiful little girl

no te preocupes — don't worry

papá — dad

perfecto — perfect

por qué — how come

qué pasa — what's wrong

te quiero — I love you

tía — aunt

tío — uncle

yo sé — I know

Talk It Out

1. Sofia wanted all the attention. Do you like being the center of attention? Why or why not?

2. Do you think Sofia's idea to use the bow was good or silly? Why?

3. Why do you think Sofia wanted to look different from her sisters?

Write It Down

1. Sofia was jealous of baby Mariela. Everyone feels jealous sometimes. Write about a time when you felt jealous.

2. Hector helped Sofia when she asked. He is a good friend to her. Write about a time when a friend helped you.

3. Pick your three favorite Spanish words or phrases from the story. Write three sentences using what you learned.

About the Author

Jacqueline Jules is the award-winning author of twenty-five children's books, including *No English* (2012 Forward National Literature Award), *Zapato Power: Freddie Ramos Takes Off* (2010 CYBILS Literary Award, Maryland Blue Crab Young Reader Honor Award, and ALSC Great Early Elementary Reads), and *Freddie Ramos Makes a Splash* (named on 2013 List of Best Children's Books of the Year by Bank Street College Committee).

When not reading, writing, or teaching, Jacqueline enjoys time with her family in Northern Virginia.

About the Illustrator

Kim Smith has worked in magazines, advertising, animation, and children's gaming. She studied illustration at the Alberta College of Art and Design in Calgary, Alberta.

Kim is the illustrator of the upcoming middle-grade mystery series *The Ghost and Max Monroe*, the picture book *Over the River and Through the Woods*, and the cover of the forthcoming middle-grade novel *How to Make a Million*. She resides in Calgary, Alberta.

FUN

doesn't stop here!

- Videos & Contests
- Games & Puzzles
- Friends & Favorites
- Authors & Illustrators

Discover more at
www.capstonekids.com

See you soon!
¡Nos Vemos pronto!